Storyteller Tales

The Crocodile Brother
and other folk tales

How can the crocodile and the duck be brothers? What happened to the greedy farmer? And how did the rabbit lose its tail?

Find out in this delightful collection of folk tales from around the world. These imaginative retellings bring the stories vividly to life and are full of action and fun.

Bob Hartman is a widely acclaimed author and storyteller. He is best known for *The Lion Storyteller Bible* and other books in the *Storyteller* series in which these tales were originally published.

The Crocodile Brother

and other folk tales

Bob Hartman

Illustrations
by Brett Hudson

A Lion Children's Book
an imprint of
Lion Hudson plc
Mayfield House, 256 Banbury Road,
Oxford OX2 7DH, England
www.lionhudson.com
ISBN 0 7459 4823 5

First edition 2004
10 9 8 7 6 5 4 3 2 1 0

Acknowledgments
These stories were first published in *The Lion Storyteller Bedtime Book* and *The Lion Storyteller Book of Animal Tales*

A catalogue record for this book is available
from the British Library

Typeset in 15/23 Baskerville MT Schlbk
Printed and bound in Great Britain
by Cox and Wyman Ltd, Reading

Contents

Silly Jack 7
A Story from England

Lazy Tom 13
A Story from Ireland

The Crocodile Brother 21
A Story from Africa

The Greedy Farmer 28
A Story from Wales

How the Rabbit Lost Its Tail 35
A Story from Japan

The Tortoise and the Hare 42
A Story from Ancient Greece

The Clever Baker 50
A Story from Scotland

The Fox and the Crow 59
A Story from Ancient Greece

Silly Jack

On Monday morning, Jack's mother sent him off to work for the carpenter. Jack worked hard, and at the end of the day the carpenter gave him a shiny new penny.

Jack carried the penny home, tossing it in the air as he went. But as he crossed the little bridge over the narrow brook, he dropped the penny and lost it in the water below.

When he told her, Jack's mother shook her

head. 'You silly boy,' she sighed, 'you should have put the penny in your pocket. You must remember that tomorrow.'

On Tuesday morning, Jack's mother sent him off to work for the farmer. Jack worked very hard, and at the end of the day the farmer gave him a jug of milk.

Jack remembered his mother's words, and carefully slipped the jug of milk into his big coat pocket. But as he walked home, the milk splashed and splooshed and spilled out of the jug and all over Jack's fine coat.

When he told her, Jack's mother shook her head. 'You silly boy,' she sighed, 'you should have carried the jug on your head. You must remember that tomorrow.'

On Wednesday morning, Jack's mother sent him off to work for the baker. Jack worked very hard, and at the end of the day, the baker gave him a beautiful black cat.

Jack remembered his mother's words, and carefully sat the cat on his head. But on the way home, the cat was frightened, leaped from Jack's head into a nearby tree, and refused to come down.

When he told her, Jack's mother shook her head. 'You silly boy,' she sighed, 'you should have tied a string around the cat's collar and pulled it home behind you. You must remember that tomorrow.'

On Thursday morning, Jack's mother sent him off to work for the butcher. Jack worked very hard, and at the end of the day, the butcher gave him a huge leg of lamb.

Jack remembered his mother's words, tied a string around the meat, and pulled it home behind him. But by the time he got home, the meat was covered with dirt, and good for nothing but to be thrown away.

When he told her, Jack's mother shook her head. 'You silly, silly boy,' she sighed. 'Don't you know you should have carried it home on your shoulder? Promise me you will remember that tomorrow.'

Jack promised, and on Friday morning, his mother sent him off to work for the man who ran the stables. Jack worked very hard, and at the end of the day, the man gave him a donkey!

Jack looked at the donkey. Jack remembered his promise. Then he swallowed hard, picked

that donkey up, and hoisted it onto his shoulders!

On the way home, Jack passed by the house of a rich man – a rich man whose beautiful daughter had never laughed in all her life.

But when she saw poor, silly Jack giving that donkey a ride, she giggled, she chuckled, then she burst out laughing, right there and then.

The rich man was delighted, and gave Jack his daughter's hand in marriage, and a huge fortune besides.

When he told her, Jack's mother didn't shake her head. No, she hugged him and she kissed him and she shouted, 'Hooray!' and she never ever called him 'silly' again.

Lazy Tom

Tom, the farmer's son, was lazy. Everybody knew it, and even he didn't mind admitting it. He knew he should have been tending to the cows, or helping out in the fields. But it was much nicer just strolling along the hedge-lined paths, chewing on a piece of straw, wasting the day away.

And then Tom heard something – a click-clacking kind of noise coming from the other side of the hedge. He thought it was a squirrel at first. Or a bird, maybe. But when it went on and on, at a strong and steady beat, he grew curious. So he crept quietly round the edge of the hedge and peeked.

It was not a squirrel. Nor any kind of bird. No, it was a tiny little man, with a leather apron hung round his neck, hammering together a wee pair of shoes.

A leprechaun! thought Tom. Here's my chance to find a fortune!

Tom moved quietly towards the little fellow, not taking his eyes off him for a second. For Tom knew that to look away from a leprechaun was to give him the chance to escape. Closer and closer Tom crept. And, what with Tom fixing his eyes on the tiny man and the click-clacking of that hammer, the leprechaun did not move an inch until Tom grabbed him with both hands and hoisted him in the air.

'Gotcha!' Tom cried. And, struggle as he might, the leprechaun could not wriggle free.

'What is it you want, then?' the leprechaun sighed. 'And be quick about it. There's work to be done. Not that you'd know anything about that,' he added. 'For if I'm not mistaken, you're Lazy Tom, the farmer's son.'

'So I am!' Tom grinned. 'But soon I shall be Rich Tom – and I won't have to lift a finger to do it – for I want nothing more or nothing less than for you to take me to your famous pot of gold!'

The leprechaun sighed again. 'Then I shall show you where it is,' he said. 'Take my hand and follow me.'

Tom set the leprechaun down, grabbed his hand and followed him through pasture and wood and stream. Finally, they came to a field covered with bright blue flowers. The leprechaun led Tom to a plant somewhere near the middle, and then he stopped.

'Dig under here,' the leprechaun said. 'And you will find my pot of gold.'

'Dig?' cried Tom. 'You said nothing about digging!'

'Well,' answered the leprechaun. 'I only promised to show you where it was. And I have done so. Now you must keep your promise and let me go!'

'All right,' replied Tom. 'But you must promise me one more thing.' And he took his handkerchief out of his pocket and tied it

round the top of the plant. 'I am going home to fetch a spade. You must promise to leave this handkerchief here until I return.'

The leprechaun looked at the handkerchief. The leprechaun looked at Tom. Then he grinned a little grin and nodded his little head.

'That I promise, as well,' he agreed. And then he disappeared.

Tom hurried back to his house, and after much asking (for he hadn't a clue where the tools were), he found a shovel. Then he hurried even more quickly back to the field. Through pasture and wood and stream he raced. He had never worked so hard in his life! But when, at last, he reached the field of bright blue flowers, he stopped his running, dropped his shovel, and stared.

The leprechaun had kept his promise. Tom's handkerchief was still tied to one of the blue flowers. But there were also handkerchiefs tied to all the other plants in that vast field – hundreds and hundreds of them, so that Tom had no idea which one belonged to him!

He could have dug them all up. But he was Lazy Tom, after all. So he shrugged his shoulders, and picked up his shovel. And, to the chirping of the birds and the chattering of the squirrels and the click-clacking of one sly little leprechaun shoemaker, he stumbled off towards home.

The Crocodile Brother

Once upon a time, there were two tribes who simply could not get along with each other. It started with a stolen cow, then a few missing pigs. Hard words followed, then threats. And when the eldest son of one of the chiefs was found murdered, everyone prepared for war!

The father of the murdered boy was broken-hearted. But in spite of his anger and his grief, the last thing he wanted was for other fathers to lose their sons as well. So he persuaded the elders of both tribes to come together and try to work out some peaceful solution.

At first, the meeting looked certain to fail.

It started with suspicious stares and soon turned into ugly shouting.

But just before the meeting fell apart completely, the chief stood and raised his hands in the air and cried, 'Crocodile!'

Everyone fell silent, each head turning this way and that, looking for the beast. And this gave the chief a chance to speak.

'There is no crocodile among us,' he said softly. 'Not yet, at least. But listen to my story, brothers, please. And perhaps you will see what I mean.

'Once there lived a crocodile,' the chief began, 'who spotted a tasty fat chicken by the side of the river. The crocodile grinned. The crocodile opened his mouth wide. The crocodile showed his rows of sharp, white teeth. But just before the crocodile snapped his jaws shut around his prey, the chicken spoke!

'"My brother," begged the chicken, "please spare my life. Find something else for your supper."

'These words surprised the crocodile. My brother? he wondered. What does the chicken mean by that? And while he wondered, the chicken slipped away.

'The next day, the crocodile spied a sleek,

juicy duck. The crocodile grinned. The crocodile opened his mouth wide. The crocodile showed his rows of sharp, white teeth. But just before the crocodile snapped his jaws shut around his prey, the duck spoke!

'"My brother," begged the duck, "please spare my life. Find something else for your supper."

'Again the crocodile was shocked. Brother? he wondered. When did I become brother to a chicken and a duck? And as he tried to puzzle it out, the duck slipped away.

'The crocodile was confused. And he was getting hungrier by the hour. So he went to see his friend, the lizard. He told him about the chicken, and he told him about the duck. And as he did so, the lizard nodded and smiled.

"“I understand completely!” answered the lizard. “For I am your brother too!”

"“My brother?” cried the crocodile. “How?”

"“I was hatched from an egg,” replied the lizard. “And so was the chicken and so was the duck.” And then he smiled at the crocodile. “And so, my brother, were you! When you think about it, we are more alike

than we ever imagined. So why should we want to eat each other?"'

His story finished, the chief turned to the elders.

'My brothers,' he said, 'we are just like that crocodile.'

'Nonsense!' called out one of the elders. 'I was never hatched from any egg!' And the elders on both sides laughed.

'No,' grinned the chief. 'But you have eyes and ears and hands and feet, as we all do. And a son – as many of us have as well. We are more alike than we ever imagined. So why should we devour one another in war, when we can live together like brothers in peace?'

The Greedy Farmer

It was nearly dark by the time poor Farmer Idris finished milking his cows. He yawned and he stretched and he made his way slowly from his ramshackle barn to his tumbledown house. Another day of hard work done – and very little to show for it.

But at the side of the cool, green lake that bordered Farmer Idris's land, another farmer's work had just begun. The sun had barely dropped behind the hills when the Fairy of the Lake walked slowly out of the water.

She was beautiful and tall, and dressed in a dripping, lake-green gown. She sang a song – the sound bubbling out of her, cool and clear as a mountain spring. And in response to that sound, a herd of pure milk-white cows came up out of the water after her and grazed on the grass at the side of the lake.

When dawn arrived, and the sun peeped its head over the hills, she returned to the water, her cows following behind. All but one, that is, who had wandered off towards Farmer Idris's house. All that day she grazed with his cows and later that evening followed them back to his barn.

Farmer Idris was surprised to see a milk-white cow among his herd. But as she had no markings and appeared to belong to no one, he kept her and milked her with the rest.

And from that moment on, the surprises never stopped! She gave more milk in one day than his whole herd could give in a week. And the taste of it – Oh! It was richer and purer than any milk he had ever drunk. There was soft, sweet butter, as well, and smooth, golden cheese, and thick, heavy cream. And people would come from miles around to smell it, to taste it and to buy it.

After many months, the milk-white cow gave birth to calves, and when they had grown, their milk was just as good as hers.

And so the years passed, the herd grew,

and poor Farmer Idris became rich Farmer Idris. And then, sadly, greedy Farmer Idris.

'The milk-white cow is growing old,' he complained to his wife, one day. 'Soon she will be no good for milking. I say we fatten her up and see how much money we can get from the butcher.'

‘But she has been such a good cow,’ his wife answered. ‘Why not let her wander the fields and graze her days away?’

‘A waste of good grass!’ Farmer Idris huffed. ‘No, we shall fatten her up. She’ll fetch good money – you’ll see.’

So that’s what Farmer Idris did. He fattened her up till she was bigger than any cow ever seen in those parts. Then he carted her off to the butcher’s – the townspeople oohing and aahing at the size and sight of her.

The butcher held her milk-white head steady. He raised his axe above her. But, just as he was about to let it fall, he heard a song echo through the valley where the little town lay. The crowd looked to the hills round about them, and there was

the Fairy of the Lake standing on the highest crag, beautiful and tall in her lake-green gown.

'Follow me, milk-white cow,' she sang. 'Come away, milk-white cow. Come with me to your home in the deep-green lake.'

Off ran the milk-white cow, galloping after the Fairy – up the hill and across the fields and towards the lake. And not only the cow, but her children and grandchildren as well – every milk-white cow in Farmer Idris's herd!

Farmer Idris ran after the cows, ran as fast as he could. And he caught up with them, just as they were walking into the lake – milk-white lilies blooming at the spot where each cow disappeared beneath the water.

He called for them. He begged them to return. He promised that the milk-white cow could graze happily on his fields for ever. But there was no answer. And soon, without his herd of fairy cows, the greedy farmer became poor Farmer Idris all over again.

How the Rabbit Lost Its Tail

Way back when the world was young, Rabbit had a long white tail!

Sometimes it dragged on the ground behind him.

Sometimes it stood straight up in the air.

But all the time, it followed Rabbit wherever he went.

One day, Rabbit wanted to visit an island, far across the sea. He curled up his tail like a

long white spring, and sat there on the beach, bouncing and thinking. But no matter how long he bounced or how hard he thought, Rabbit could not find a way to get across the water.

Then, a shark swam by. And suddenly, Rabbit had an idea. A sneaky idea, for Rabbit was quite a trickster.

'Excuse me, Shark,' he called. 'I was just sitting here, bouncing and thinking – and

I wondered – how many friends does a shark have?'

'Friends?' Shark replied. 'Hundreds and hundreds, I should think.'

'I'm surprised!' said Rabbit. 'I always thought that sharks were quite fierce and lonely creatures.'

'A common mistake,' Shark grinned, his bright white teeth gleaming in the sunlight. 'We're really very friendly, and only show our fierce side when something makes us angry. Let me show you.'

And with that, Shark disappeared beneath the surface of the water. But, when he came up again, he was not alone. There were hundreds of sharks, grinning behind him, stretched out across the water, as far as Rabbit could see!

'I'm impressed!' said Rabbit. 'So many friends! Would you mind if I counted them?'

'Of course not,' grinned Shark. 'Do what you like. It will only prove my point.'

So Rabbit counted the sharks. He hopped onto their heads, one by one, counting them as he went.

He hopped on ten sharks and twenty sharks and thirty sharks.

He hopped on forty sharks and fifty sharks and sixty sharks.

He hopped on seventy sharks and

eighty sharks and ninety sharks.

And when he had hopped onto a hundred sharks, Rabbit just kept hopping – until he had hopped on the heads of three hundred sharks.

And then, Rabbit hopped onto the island!

'So have I made my point?' asked Shark, who had been swimming alongside Rabbit, all the while.

'Absolutely!' Rabbit chuckled.

'Then what's so funny?' asked Shark.

Rabbit chuckled again. And then, because

he found it impossible to keep a good trick to himself, he went on.

'Well, I really couldn't care less how many friends you have. I just needed a way to cross the sea!'

Then Rabbit turned to walk away from the beach, his long tail dancing behind him. But Shark did not turn away. No, he did not like being tricked and was angry at Rabbit for making a fool of him and his friends. So, as Rabbit turned, Shark leaped out of the water and, flashing his sharp teeth, bit off Rabbit's long white tail.

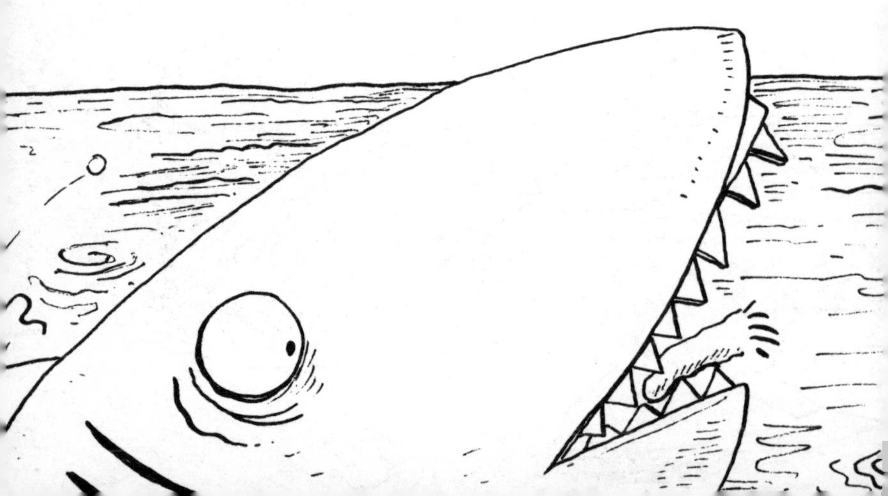

'Yowch!' cried Rabbit, running off into the woods – his tail now no more than a little white tuft of a thing.

But did that teach him a lesson? Did it cure Rabbit of his trickster ways? It did not.

For when it came time to leave the island, Rabbit sat on the beach again. And simply waited until he found a fish with more friends than teeth!

The Tortoise and the Hare

Tortoise was slow. Very slow.

He walked slowly. And he talked slowly. And when he ate his dinner, he chewed each bite slowly, a hundred times or more.

Hare, however, was fast. Very fast.

He never walked anywhere. He ran.

He talked so quickly that his friends hardly understood what he said.

And as for his dinner – well, he gobbled

it down before anyone else could even start.

Hare liked to laugh at Tortoise.

'Slowcoach.' That's what he called him. And 'Slow-mo' and 'Mr Slowy Slow'.

Tortoise put up with this for a long time (he was slow to get angry as well). But one day, Tortoise had had enough. So he turned to Hare and said (very slowly, of course), 'Why don't you race me, then?'

Hare fell over in fits of laughter. He giggled and snorted and chuckled and guffawed, all in one quick breath.

'Of course I'll race you!' he answered. 'I'll run so fast you won't even see me!'

The day of the race arrived, and Hare's friends gathered round to cheer him on.

'I'll beat him! I'll crush him! I'll run him into the ground!' chattered Hare. And he spoke so quickly that all his friends could answer was:

'Eh?'

And 'Huh?'

And 'What did he say?'

But they clapped him on the back and cheered anyway.

There was no one, however, to support Tortoise, because no one wanted to be seen with a loser.

So he waited patiently at the starting line, slowly stretching one leg and then another, hoping to avoid any painful tortoise cramps.

At last, someone shouted, 'Ready. Steady. Go!'

Hare leaped from the line and raced off so quickly that he soon disappeared over the first hill. But Tortoise just plodded slowly along – one foot in front of the other – determined to do his best.

Mile after mile flashed by as Hare raced past cars and motorbikes and trains.

And Tortoise plodded on, step by slow step, stopping now and then to give way to the odd, passing snail.

In no time at all, the finishing line was

in Hare's sight. A crowd of animals was on the other side, waiting to cheer his victory. But instead of rushing over it, he decided to have one last laugh at Tortoise's expense.

He waved to the crowd, pointed to a shady tree and then settled down for a little nap.

'I'll show them,' he chuckled. 'I can sleep half the day and still beat that slowcoach!'

So Hare fell asleep, while Tortoise plodded on.

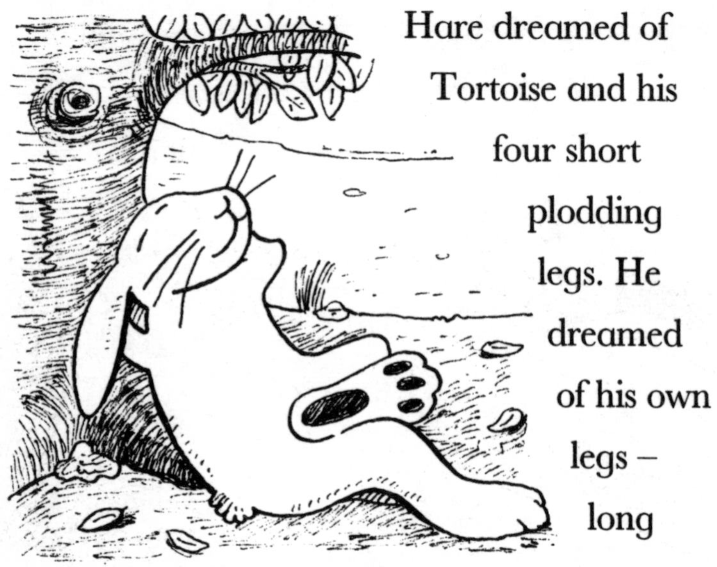

Hare dreamed of Tortoise and his four short plodding legs. He dreamed of his own legs – long and strong and fast. Then he dreamed of the race and the finishing line and the cheering crowds. And then, suddenly, he was dreaming no longer. He was awake! But the crowds were, somehow, still cheering.

Hare opened his eyes and peered at the crowd. They were shouting and raising their hands in the air. But how could that be? He was still under the tree. And that's when Hare saw Tortoise – only a short step away from the finishing line! And then Hare looked at the sun. It had almost dipped

below the hills, for with all his dreaming he had slept the day away!

Hare leaped to his feet. He raced. He rushed. He fairly flew. But Tortoise just kept plodding. And even though Hare strained every last muscle in his long strong legs, Tortoise managed to plod over the line just a step ahead!

'It's not fair!' chattered Hare. 'I was there! By the tree! You all saw me!'

'Eh?' said the crowd.

And 'Huh?'

And 'What did he say?'

Then everyone rushed to Tortoise and lifted him in the air, cheering and shouting his name. While Hare was left alone, huffing and puffing and complaining away, nursing one painful hare cramp!

The Clever Baker

Annie was a baker – the best in all Scotland. Shortbreads and buns and cakes – she made them all. And they were so delicious that no one ever left a crumb behind, on table or plate or floor.

Now this was fine for everyone but the fairies, who depended on those crumbs, and who had never had so much as a tiny taste of one of Annie's famous cakes. So one bright morning, the Fairy King decided to do something about that. He hid himself among the wild flowers by the side of the road, and when Annie passed on her way to market, he sprinkled fairy dust in her eyes to make her fall fast asleep.

When Annie awoke, she was no longer on the road, but deep in fairyland, face to face with the Fairy King.

'Annie!' the King commanded. 'Everyone has tasted your wonderful cakes. Everyone, but us! So from now on, you will stay here in fairyland and bake for us every day.'

Oh dear, thought Annie. But she didn't show that she was worried, or even scared, for she was a clever woman. No, she set her mind, at once, to making a plan for her escape.

'Very well,' she said, 'But if I am to bake you a cake, I will need ingredients – flour and milk, eggs and sugar and butter.'

'Fetch them at once!' commanded the Fairy King. So off the fairies flew, to Annie's house. And back they flew, in a flash, with everything she needed.

'Oh dear,' Annie sighed, shaking her head

(and still without a plan). 'If I am to bake a cake, I will also need my tools – my pots and pans and pitchers and bowls and spoons.'

'Fetch them, quickly!' the Fairy King commanded again. But when the fairies returned, they were in such a hurry that they stumbled and sent the pots and pans crashing and clanking across the floor.

'OOH! OWW!' cried the Fairy King, jamming his hands against his ears. 'You know very well that I cannot stand loud noises!'

And, at that moment, Annie had her plan.

She broke the eggs and poured the milk and mixed in the flour and butter. But when she stirred the batter, she made the spoon clatter – clackety, clackety, clack – against the side of the bowl.

The Fairy King winced at the noise, but Annie could see that it was not loud enough. And so she said, 'Oh dear. I am used to having my little yellow cat beside me when I bake. I cannot make my best cake unless he is here.'

So the Fairy King commanded, and the fairies went, and came back at once with the cat.

Annie put the cat under the table and, as

she mixed the batter, she trod, ever so gently, on the cat's tail.

And so the spoon went, 'Clackety, clackety, clack!'

And the cat went, 'Yow! Yow! Yow!'

And the Fairy King looked even more uncomfortable.

'Oh dear,' said Annie again. 'It's still not right. I'm also used to having my big brown dog beside me when I bake. I don't suppose…?'

'Yes, yes,' sighed the Fairy King. 'Anything for a taste of that cake.'

And the fairies were sent for the dog.

Annie put him next to the cat, and he soon began to bark.

And so the spoon went, 'Clackety, clackety, clack!'

And the cat went, 'Yow! Yow! Yow!'

And the dog went, 'Woof! Woof! Woof!'

And the Fairy King stuck a fairy finger in one ear.

'Just one more thing,' said Annie. 'I am worried about my little baby. And I cannot do my best work when I am worried.'

'All right, all right,' moaned the Fairy King.

And he sent off his fairies one more time.

The baby was asleep when she arrived, but as soon as she heard all the noise, she awoke with a cry.

And so the spoon went, 'Clackety, clackety, clack!'

And the cat went, 'Yow! Yow! Yow!'

And the dog went, 'Woof! Woof! Woof!'

And the baby went, 'Wah! Wah! Wah!'

And the Fairy King put his hands over his ears and shouted, 'Enough! Enough! Enough!'

And everything went quiet.

'Even the best cake in the world is not worth this racket,' he cried. 'Take your baby, Woman, and your dog and your cat and your noisy spoon. Go back to your own world, and leave us in peace!'

Annie smiled. 'I'll do better than that,' she said. 'If you promise to leave me be, I'll put a special little cake for you and your people by the fairy mound each day.'

'That's a bargain,' smiled the Fairy King, and Annie and all that belonged to her were returned to her kitchen in a flash.

And every day, from then on, Annie left a little cake by the fairy mound. And the Fairy King not only left her alone; each day he left her a little bag of gold, where the cake had been. And they all lived happily ever after.

The Fox and the Crow

Fox crept slowly – crept up on Crow.

But as he sprang into the air – red fur flying and white teeth flashing – Crow flew away into the branches of a tall tree.

It was not Crow that Fox wanted, but the fat piece of cheese she held in her beak. So he stood thinking for a moment, and, when he had come up with another plan, Fox trotted towards the tree and called to

Crow in his most pleasant voice, 'Crow! Dear Crow, I'm sorry I startled you. I was just overcome, that's all.'

Overcome? wondered Crow silently. And she stared at Fox, confused.

'How else can I put it?' Fox said. 'It is rare that one stumbles upon such beauty as yours in this rough and ordinary world.'

Crow stared, more puzzled than ever. Beauty? Me? she wondered. And she went to fly away.

'I can tell by your expression,' Fox continued, 'that you are not following my meaning. Stay with me, just a moment, and I will explain.

'I have seen crows before. Many crows, in fact. But none with such shiny feathers as yours. None with such shapely wings.

And certainly none with such deep black eyes.'

Crow could not hide her pleasure! This was all a surprise to her. But a wonderful surprise, to be sure. She wanted to say, 'Go on. More please!' But there was the cheese to consider and, besides, Fox showed no signs of stopping!

'It is not only your appearance that has touched me,' he went on, 'but your considerable talent as well. Most birds of your kind would have launched themselves clumsily from the ground. But you soared! The graceful arc of your wings was a picture – no, a poem! – against the evening sky!'

Crow was trembling now, overwhelmed by Fox's flattery. And so she was totally unprepared for what came next.

'Dare I say it?' Fox whispered. 'Is it too much to hope for? But is it possible, just possible, that flying is not your only gift? Is it possible that you can also… sing?

'If so, then I would love nothing more than to hear you. Could you…? Would you… (Dare I even suggest such a thing?) honour me with just one note from that lovely crow throat?'

Crow could no longer think. She was so taken in by Fox's sweet words that she forgot even the simplest thing – that crows cannot sing. Not even one note.

So Crow opened her mouth, and two things happened.

The most awful 'squawk' came out of her beak. And the cheese came out as well!

In fact, it dropped straight to the ground, where Fox gobbled it down in one bite.

'Thank you very kindly,' he grinned. 'I knew something wonderful would come out of that mouth of yours.'

Then he trotted off into the forest, leaving Crow feeling foolish and flattered all at the same time.

A Note from the Author

As you may wish to read other versions of some of these traditional stories, I would like to acknowledge some of the sources I have referred to, although most of these stories can be found in several collections.

'Lazy Tom' from 'The Field of Boliauns' in *Fairy Tales from the British Isles* by A. Williams-Ellis, Frederick Warne & Co., London. 'The Crocodile Brother' from *Zoo of the Gods*, Anthony S. Mercatante, Harper and Row, New York, 1974. 'The Greedy Farmer' from 'The Marvellous Cow of Clyn Barfog' in *Elves and Ellefolk* by N.M. Belting, Holt, Rinehart and Winston, New York. 'How the Rabbit Lost Its Tail' from *Little One-Inch and Other Japanese Children's Favorite Stories*, ed. Florence Sakade, Charles E. Tuttle Company, Rutland, Vermont, 1984. 'The Tortoise and the Hare' and 'The Fox and the Crow' from *Aesop*, or from *The Fables of La Fontaine*, Richard Scarry, Doubleday and Company Inc., Garden City, New York, 1963. 'The Clever Baker' from 'The Woman Who Flummoxed the Fairies' in *Heather and Broom* by S.N. Leodhas, Holt, Rinehart and Winston, New York.